I SPY

SUPER CHALLENGER!

A BOOK OF PICTURE RIDDLES

Photographs by Walter Wick

Riddles by Jean Marzollo

Cartwheel ·B·O·O·K·S· ®

SCHOLASTIC INC.

New York   Toronto   London   Auckland   Sydney
Mexico City   New Delhi   Hong Kong   Buenos Aires

For Zoë and Eva Morozko

W.W.

For Ricky
and Zhao Hong

J.M.

Go to www.scholastic.com for Web site information
on Scholastic authors and illustrators.

Book design by Carol Devine Carson

Library of Congress Cataloging-in-Publication Data

Wick, Walter.
    I spy super challenger: a book of picture riddles / photographs by Walter Wick; riddles by
Jean Marzollo
        p.   cm.085. — (I spy)
    ISBN 0-590-34128-6
    1. Picture puzzles—Juvenile literature.   2. Riddles—Juvenile literature.   I. Marzollo, Jean.   II. Title.
III. Series.
GV1507.P47W5295   1997
793.735—dc21   97-6864
                                                                                           CIP
                                                                                            AC

ISBN-13: 978-0-590-34128-8
ISBN-10: 0-590-34128-6

51 50 49 48 47   24 25 26 27 28

Printed in China   38
First printing, September 1997

TABLE OF CONTENTS

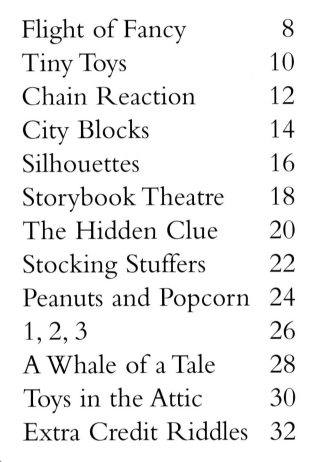

Flight of Fancy 8

Tiny Toys 10

Chain Reaction 12

City Blocks 14

Silhouettes 16

Storybook Theatre 18

The Hidden Clue 20

Stocking Stuffers 22

Peanuts and Popcorn 24

1, 2, 3 26

A Whale of a Tale 28

Toys in the Attic 30

Extra Credit Riddles 32

Picture riddles fill this book;
Turn the pages! Take a look!

Use your mind, use your eye;
Read the riddles—play I SPY!

I spy a hydrant, an iron, a dart,

Two cowboy boots, a little glass heart;

Three birds, a bell, a beetle, a B,
A flame, and the Roman numeral III.

I spy three dogs, two cleaners for pipes,
A baby asleep, the Stars and Stripes;

Eyes with no face, a fireman's axe,
A trotting globe, and ten little jacks.

I spy two ladders, a duck and its twin,

A mousetrap, a sailor, a tiny clothespin;

A candle, a pipe, a watchband, a ball,
And a towering clown who will soon take a fall.

I spy a limo, a mouse, and a rock,

Two bows, a boat, a bee on a block;

A pencil, a golf tee, a church with a cross,
A jingle bell, and chocolate sauce.

15

I spy a penguin, a fine-tooth comb,
A zipper pull tab, and a little bird's home;

A cone from a sweetshop, a cone from a tree,
A bow tie, a tiger, a mouse, and a G.

I spy an apple, a house of bricks,

Four candy canes, and eight craft sticks;

An owl, a dragon, a cricket, a bee,
Musical notes, and the number three.

I spy two spurs, two dogs, two 8's,
Four red hands, four tops, two skates;

An off-on switch, a see-through trunk,
A paper clip, and a statue that shrunk.

I spy two snowmen, a walnut, a horn,
Paper-clip skates, an ear of corn;

A birthday candle, a brown-and-white dog,
A cricket, a soccer ball, and a hog.

23

I spy a bat, a balloon, a pail,

A box of potatoes, a horse's tail;

Two umbrellas, a little spare tire,
A baby bottle, ICE, and Fire.

I spy a nut, thirteen number nines,
Twenty-five spades, and three road signs;

Two pennies, two cacti, four arrows, a stork,
Six dominoes, five flags, and a fork.

I spy three clothespins, a fast-riding man,
A wooden heart, and a watering can;

A safety pin, a shiny blue hat,
A rat, a cat, a bat, and ALL THAT.

I spy a pumpkin, a white wooden chair,

Miss LAZYBONES, and a boot in the air;

A running dish, a hammer, a plane,
And hardest of all, a PAGE with a train.

EXTRA CREDIT RIDDLES

Find the Pictures That Go With These Riddles:

I spy an acorn, a telephone toy,

A key, and an angel drummer boy.

I spy a rainbow, a bird that is blue,

Ballet slippers, and binoculars, too.

I spy a blue boot, a small fish with fins,

A jump rope, and ten white bowling pins.

I spy a sea horse, teeth, and a V,

A domino, and a wooden D.

I spy a flag and a small puzzle piece,

Three barrels, two hens, and worn-out fleece.

I spy a peeking giraffe, a truck,

Six red shoes, and a little blue duck.

I spy a knight, four pigs' tails,

Two scary wolves, and two little pails.

I spy a taxi, a woman with a cane,

A domino, eight black dots near a plane.

I spy a horseshoe, a broom, four B's,

OIL, eight crab legs, and three little trees.

I spy a strainer, the point of a pen,

A wrench, a zebra, and three sportsmen.

I spy three mice, a tortoise, a hare,

An itchy colt, and a climbing bear.

I spy a sandal, a game-board shoe,

A grand piano, and Pegasus, too.

Write Your Own Picture Riddles

There are many more hidden objects and many more possibilities for riddles in this book. Write some rhyming picture riddles yourself, and try them out with friends.

About the Creators of *I Spy*

Jean Marzollo has written many rhyming children's books including the I Spy books, *Ten Cats Have Hats*, *Pretend You're a Cat*, *Home Sweet Home*, and *Sun Song*. She is the author of acclaimed nonfiction for children including *I Am Water*, *In 1492*, and *Happy Birthday, Martin Luther King*, and popular books for beginning readers including *Football Friends* and *Soccer Cousins*. For nineteen years, Jean Marzollo and Carol Carson produced Scholastic's kindergarten magazine, *Let's Find Out*. Ms. Marzollo holds a master's degree from the Harvard Graduate School of Education. She lives with her husband, Claudio, in Cold Spring, New York.

Walter Wick is the photographer of seven previous I Spy books including *I Spy: A Book of Picture Riddles*, *I Spy Christmas*, *I Spy Fun House*, and *I Spy Spooky Night* and is both author and photographer of *A Drop of Water: A Book of Science and Wonder*, which has garnered high praise from reviewers. Prior to creating children's books, Mr. Wick invented photographic games for *Games* magazine and photographed more than 300 covers for books and magazines, including *Newsweek*, *Discover*, *Psychology Today*, and Scholastic's *Let's Find Out* and *Super Science*. Mr. Wick is a graduate of Paier College of Art. He lives with his wife, Linda, in New York and Connecticut.

Carol Devine Carson, the book designer for the I Spy series, is art director for a major publishing house in New York City.

The Story of *I Spy Super Challenger*

For years children who have found every single thing in every single *I Spy* book have begged for a harder book to challenge their visual and mental skills. Consequently, Walter Wick and Jean Marzollo selected from previous *I Spy* books the hardest pictures—the ones with the most objects. Jean Marzollo then asked children in second and third grade to tell her which objects were the most difficult to find. With their comments and eager spirit in mind, she wrote brand new rhyming riddles. Warning to grown-ups: if this book is too hard for you, enlist some children to help.

Acknowledgments

We'd like to thank the many children and their teachers who tested these riddles for us: William, Isaac, Tommi Ann, Alessandra, Rebecca, Geoffrey, Chad, Ian, Tom, Amanda, Robbie, Jeff, Caitlin, Laila, Owen, and Mrs. Donna Norkeliunas; Kerry, Dani, Ryan, David, Sasha, Sam, Ray, Matt W., Lucas, Maike, Jo, Desi, Lana, Kim, Erica, Marty, Billy, Sophie, Rachael, Matt H., Jasen, Matt A., and Ms. Brennan; Jordan, Lee, Justine, Erin, Ryan, Adrienne, Brandon, Katie, Hannah, and Greyson. We'd also like to thank David Marzollo for his outstanding creative input.

Jean Marzollo and Walter Wick

I Spy Books for All Ages:
I SPY: A BOOK OF PICTURE RIDDLES
I SPY CHRISTMAS
I SPY EXTREME CHALLENGER!
I SPY FANTASY
I SPY FUN HOUSE
I SPY GOLD CHALLENGER!
I SPY MYSTERY
I SPY SCHOOL DAYS
I SPY SPOOKY NIGHT
I SPY SUPER CHALLENGER!
I SPY TREASURE HUNT
I SPY ULTIMATE CHALLENGER!
I SPY YEAR-ROUND CHALLENGER!

Books for New Readers:
SCHOLASTIC READER LVL 1: I SPY A BALLOON
SCHOLASTIC READER LVL 1: I SPY A BUTTERFLY
SCHOLASTIC READER LVL 1: I SPY A CANDY CANE
SCHOLASTIC READER LVL 1: I SPY A DINOSAUR'S EYE
SCHOLASTIC READER LVL 1: I SPY A PENGUIN
SCHOLASTIC READER LVL 1: I SPY A PUMPKIN
SCHOLASTIC READER LVL 1: I SPY A SCARY MONSTER
SCHOLASTIC READER LVL 1: I SPY A SCHOOL BUS
SCHOLASTIC READER LVL 1: I SPY FUNNY TEETH
SCHOLASTIC READER LVL 1: I SPY LIGHTNING IN THE SKY
SCHOLASTIC READER LVL 1: I SPY SANTA CLAUS

And for the Youngest Child:
I SPY LITTLE ANIMALS
I SPY LITTLE BOOK
I SPY LITTLE BUNNIES
I SPY LITTLE CHRISTMAS
I SPY LITTLE LEARNING BOX
I SPY LITTLE LETTERS
I SPY LITTLE NUMBERS
I SPY LITTLE WHEELS

Also Available:
I SPY CHALLENGER FOR GAME BOY ADVANCE
I SPY JUNIOR: PUPPET PLAYHOUSE CD-ROM
I SPY JUNIOR CD-ROM
I SPY SCHOOL DAYS CD-ROM
I SPY SPOOKY MANSION CD-ROM
I SPY TREASURE HUNT CD-ROM